NEW POEMS

By the same author

Poetry
THE WANDERING ISLANDS
POEMS
SELECTED POEMS (Australian Poets Series)
COLLECTED POEMS 1930-1965

Criticism
THE CAVE AND THE SPRING
NATIVE COMPANIONS (in preparation)

A. D. HOPE

NEW POEMS

1965-1969

NEW YORK　THE VIKING PRESS

Copyright © 1968, 1969 by A. D. Hope

All rights reserved

Published in 1970 by The Viking Press, Inc.
625 Madison Avenue, New York, N.Y. 10022

Published simultaneously in Canada by
The Macmillan Company of Canada Limited

Library of Congress catalog card number: 72-94856

PRINTED IN AUSTRALIA

ACKNOWLEDGMENTS

POEMS in this collection that have previously been published elsewhere are: "Lament for the Murderers" in *The Bulletin*, "On an Engraving by Casserius" in *The Hudson Review* and *The Bulletin*, "Loving Kind" in *Poetry Magazine*, "The Apotelesm of W. B. Yeats" and "The School of Night" in *Poetry* and *Quadrant*, "Advice to a Poet" in *Spirit*, "A Visit to the Ruins" in *Quadrant*, "Sonnets to Baudelaire" in *Southerly* and *Partisan Review*.

CONTENTS

1965
Argolis — 1

1966
Lament for the Murderers — 2

1967
The Planctus — 4
Paradise Saved — 9
Moschus Moschiferus — 10
On an Engraving by Casserius — 12
Loving Kind — 17

1968
The Apotelesm of W. B. Yeats — 18
Tiger — 19
Advice to a Poet — 21
A Visit to the Ruins — 23
Sonnets to Baudelaire — 25
"With Thee Conversing..." — 32
Six Songs for Chloë — 33
   I The Vintage — 33
   II The Perfume — 35
   III Going to Bed — 37
   IV The Quarrel — 39
   V The Lamp — 41
   VI The Lunch — 43
The School of Night — 47

Lieder ohne Buchstaben 49
When Like the Sun . . . 51

1969
As Well as They Can 52
The Great Baboons 53
Vivaldi, Bird and Angel 59
Notes 75

ARGOLIS

Home the farmer carts his sheaves,
Homeward rides a laurelled brow:
Living bread and barren leaves,
Yet the sword puts down the plough.

Harvest home for man and beast,
Rustic dance and country mirth
While the soldier's drunken feast
Triumphs on a plundered hearth.

Till by blackened walls a shape
Crumbles where the reaper died
And the soldier gorged with rape
Bleeds upon the reaper's bride.

Winter comes to heap the snow
High on the abandoned shield,
Spring to find the rusting plough
Deep in thistles by the field.

In the ether calm and wise
Zeus surveys the fates of men
And ordains their world to rise
From its ruins once again.

Deep beneath a broken land
Grim Hephaestus, at his word,
Forging with impartial hand,
Sets the ploughshare by the sword.

LAMENT FOR THE MURDERERS

Where are they now, the genteel murderers
And gentlemanly sleuths, whose household names
Made crime a club for well-bred amateurs;
Slaughter the cosiest of indoor games?

Where are the long week-ends, the sleepless nights
We spent treading the dance in dead men's shoes,
And all the ratiocinative delights
Of matching motives and unravelling clues,

The public-spirited corpse in evening dress,
Blood like an order across the snowy shirt,
Killings contrived with no unseemly mess
And only rank outsiders getting hurt:

A fraudulent banker or a blackmailer,
The rich aunt dragging out her spiteful life,
The lovely bitch, the cheap philanderer
Bent on seducing someone else's knife?

Where are those headier methods of escape
From the dull fare of peace: the well-spiced dish
Of torture, violence and brutal rape,
Perversion, madness and still queerer fish?

All gone! That dear delicious make-believe,
The armchair blood-sports and dare-devil dreams.
We dare not even sleep now, dare not leave
The armchair. What we hear are real screams.

Real people, whom we know, have really died.
No one knows why. The nightmares have come true.
We ring the police: A voice says "Homicide!
Just wait your turn. When we get round to you

You will be sorry you were born. Don't call
For help again: a murderer saves his breath.
When guilt consists in being alive at all
Justice becomes the other name for Death."

THE PLANCTUS

Do quietem fidibus;
vellem ut et planctibus
sic possem et fletibus.

                        Abelard: *Planctus 6, IV, B.*

I

Time be my Fulbert, history your Paraclete,
And Astrolabe though yours, not mine, alas!
Those two our palimpsest, we their looking-glass,
In essence, if not in accidents, complete;
No detail matches, yet the patterns repeat:
Thrice crows the cock as introit to the mass;
Buridan in his sack sees Buridan's ass
Stuck between wild oats and domestic wheat.

Were all their letters genuine? Who can tell?
Though ours authenticate the text at need,
Christ's cross for Adam's tree no more stands bail.

Tell-tale, tell-tale, tell-tale! tolls the bell,
While bill-boards outside Paradise now read:
"This Most Desirable Property, for Sale!"

II

The Faith is dead; the men are gone; their graves
Remain: these two byzantine churches and
The bones of those who built them. Silt and sand
Choked this proud city whose life was from the waves.

Lost Adam, lost Eve from a lost world, the nave's
Mosaics show us naked, hand in hand,
Fixed where now only tourists drift or stand,
The culture-addicts and the camera-slaves.

Who will remember our city in its grace?
Only ourselves, survivors, each inside
A separate ark, lost on the endless flood,
Posting each other at random on the wide
Waste waters, raven or dove to ask: What good
Will Ararat be, if Babel takes its place?

III

Angels of stone, great mountains, flash their brands
Of lightning round St Peter's tower, whose stone
Was cut when Peter, Berengarius' son
Was born; a house of grief not made with hands,
Set on that rock, is now my house; his lands
Of exile I inherit; the *Sic et Non*
Of mind and heart drags on; I sit alone
Petrus in vinculis ...
                          suddenly his bands
Lie loose; a voice dispels the prisoner's sleep;
Domine suo ... writes Heloissa's pen;
A *trouvère's* aubade finds his exiled King,
The lion-heart fretting in the Styrian Keep,
And this grey hillside glows as bright as spring
With autumn crocus and wild cyclamen.

IV

A horror of great darkness, in that dark
The furnace and the lamp between the slain
And, lastly, the Shekinah shining plain
Upon the friend of God, the patriarch.

I know the horror: I cannot find the friend;
I see the mysteries, but I miss the light.
Bear with me now: against myself I fight:
Cannot go on, yet cannot make an end.

His enemies, when he visited her would laugh
And say: the old Adam draws him to her still!
Fierce in his right, he gave them all the lie.
Had he been in my case, had he known half
The agony of my divided will
Lama sabachthani must have been his cry.

V

My plane comes in to land and now I see
As angels on their errands see, the bay,
And Palo Alto and the Royal Way,
The hills beyond where grew our fatal tree.
Almost I could believe we stand there now
In that first flash of vision, when the eyes
Take in what still they cannot realize,
Our fingers meeting round its golden bough.

Ten years ago! A sorry angel, I
Too late to an abandoned hearth descend.
The Palatine Peripatetic, having come
To such a point as this wrote: When I die,
No matter where, for my poor body send.
To that at least I shall not grudge its home!

VI

Dimisit eam: knowing it was too late
He preached on these two words from Genesis.
Abraham loved Sara still, he said, but his
Whole soul was Agar's, and, as they relate,
Having driven her out to satisfy the Lord,
His heart rebelled and, grim for her distress,
He ran to find her in the wilderness,
And met an angel with a flaming sword

Who said: Turn back! This desert was Paradise.
But showed him by a well where Agar slept
Safe with her child. Far off a ghost crowed thrice.
Because he loved her more than all beside,
There Abraham fell upon his face and wept.
But Peter faced the brethren stony-eyed.

VII

In his last years, they say, a gentleness
Fell on this second Petrus, this rolling stone,
On whom, for all that, Thomas built the throne
Of doctrine. Peter of Cluny none the less
Was not deceived by this apparent peace.
He mourns beside the Burning Bush, he said,
That was his love. And, when the man was dead,
He sent the body back to Héloïse.

I am not gentle; I know (I shall not yield)
Time's rage; the cock may crow: I cannot weep;
This body rebels and lives, but moves apart
Not towards its Paraclete, but some Potter's Field.
Yet in your unconsuming flame, this heart
Rejoices and this spirit you have and keep.

VIII

Near death at St Marcel, he loosed his tongue:
Once when they asked his age, he said: I am
Older than wandering Caym, than Abraham
When he betrayed his love. . . . Yet I am young!
Seven years for Leah—they were years, no more,
The seven for Rachel were the seven days
Of the Creation, the renewal of grace
In that new testament beyond the law.

The seven that followed, and all that follow those
Cannot be told for they are not in time
But in the eternal sabbaths of the song
I sent her for her nuns; for that I chose
A metre from the love-songs of my prime
Since in that heaven of heavens all things belong.

Quis rex, quae curia, quale palatium,
Quae pax, quae requies, quod illud gaudium,
Hujus participes exponant gloriae,
Si quantum sentiunt possint exprimere.

IX (Epigraph)

PARADISE SAVED

(another version of the Fall)

Adam, indignant, would not eat with Eve,
They say, and she was driven from his side.
Watching the gates close on her tears, his pride
Upheld him, though he could not help but grieve

And climbed the wall, because his loneliness
Pined for her lonely figure in the dust:
Lo, there were two! God who is more than just
Sent her a helpmeet in that wilderness.

Day after day he watched them in the waste
Grow old, breaking the harsh unfriendly ground,
Bearing their children, till at last they died;
While Adam, whose fellow God had not replaced,
Lived on immortal, young, with virtue crowned,
Sterile and impotent and justified.

MOSCHUS MOSCHIFERUS

A Song for St Cecilia's Day

In the high jungle where Assam meets Tibet
The small Kastura, most archaic of deer,
Were driven in herds to cram the hunters' net
And slaughtered for the musk-pods which they bear;

But in those thickets of rhododendron and birch
The tiny creatures now grow hard to find.
Fewer and fewer survive each year. The search
Employs new means, more exquisite and refined:

The hunters now set out by two or three;
Each carries a bow and one a slender flute.
Deep in the forest the archers choose a tree
And climb; the piper squats against the root.

And there they wait until all trace of man
And rumour of his passage dies away.
They melt into the leaves and, while they scan
The glade below, their comrade starts to play.

Through those vast listening woods a tremulous skein
Of melody wavers, delicate and shrill:
Now dancing and now pensive, now a rain
Of pure, bright drops of sound and now the still,

Sad wailing of lament; from tune to tune
It winds and modulates without a pause;
The hunters hold their breath; the trance of noon
Grows tense; with its full power the music draws

A shadow from a juniper's darker shade;
Bright-eyed, with quivering muzzle and pricked ear,
The little musk-deer slips into the glade
Led by an ecstasy that conquers fear.

A wild enchantment lures him, step by step,
Into its net of crystalline sound, until
The leaves stir overhead, the bowstrings snap
And poisoned shafts bite sharp into the kill.

Then, as the victim shudders, leaps and falls,
The music soars to a delicious peak,
And on and on its silvery piping calls
Fresh spoil for the rewards the hunters seek.

But when the woods are emptied and the dusk
Draws in, the men climb down and count their prey,
Cut out the little glands that hold the musk
And leave the carcasses to rot away.

A hundred thousand or so are killed each year;
Cause and effect are very simply linked:
Rich scents demand the musk, and so the deer,
Its source, must soon, they say, become extinct.

Divine Cecilia, there is no more to say!
Of all who praised the power of music, few
Knew of these things. In honour of your day
Accept this song I too have made for you.

ON AN ENGRAVING BY CASSERIUS
For Dr John Z. Bowers

Set on this bubble of dead stone and sand,
Lapped by its frail balloon of lifeless air,
Alone in the inanimate void, they stand,
These clots of thinking molecules who stare
Into the night of nescience and death,
And, whirled about with their terrestrial ball,
Ask of all being its motion and its frame:
This of all human images takes my breath;
Of all the joys in being a man at all,
This folds my spirit in its quickening flame.

Turning the leaves of this majestic book
My thoughts are with those great cosmographers,
Surgeon adventurers who undertook
To probe and chart time's other universe.
This one engraving holds me with its theme:
More than all maps made in that century
Which set true bearings for each cape and star,
De Quiros' vision or Newton's cosmic dream,
This reaches towards the central mystery
Of whence our being draws and what we are.

It came from that great school in Padua:
Casserio and Spiegel made this page.
Vesalius, who designed the *Fabrica*,
There strove, but burned his book at last in rage;
Fallopius by its discipline laid bare
The elements of this humanity,
Without which none knows that which treats the soul;
Fabricius talked with Galileo there:
Did those rare spirits in their colloquy
Divine in their two skills the single goal?

"One force that moves the atom and the star,"
Says Galileo; "one basic law beneath
All change!" "Would light from Achernar
Reveal how embryon forms within its sheath?"
Fabricius asks, and smiles. Talk such as this,
Ranging the bounds of our whole universe,
Could William Harvey once have heard? And once
Hearing, strike out that strange hypothesis,
Which in *De Motu Cordis* twice recurs,
Coupling the heart's impulsion with the sun's?

Did Thomas Browne at Padua, too, in youth
Hear of their talk of universal law
And form that notion of particular truth
Framed to correct a science they foresaw,
That darker science of which he used to speak
In later years and called the Crooked Way
Of Providence? Did *he* foresee perhaps
An age in which all sense of the unique,
And singular dissolves, like ours today,
In diagrams, statistics, tables, maps?

Not here! The graver's tool in this design
Aims still to give not general truth alone,
Blue-print of science or data's formal line:
Here in its singularity he has shown
The image of an individual soul;
Bodied in this one woman, he makes us see
The shadow of his anatomical laws.
An artist's vision animates the whole,
Shines through the scientist's detailed scrutiny
And links the person and the abstract cause.

Such were the charts of those who pressed beyond
Vesalius their master, year by year
Tracing each bone, each muscle, every frond
Of nerve until the whole design lay bare.
Thinking of this dissection, I descry
The tiers of faces, their teacher in his place,
The talk at the cadaver carried in:
"A woman—with child!"; I hear the master's dry
Voice as he lifts a scalpel from its case:
"With each new step in science, we begin."

Who was she? Though they never knew her name,
Dragged from the river, found in some alley at dawn,
This corpse none cared, or dared perhaps, to claim;
The dead child in her belly still unborn,
Might have passed, momentary as a shooting star,
Quenched like the misery of her personal life,
Had not the foremost surgeon of Italy,
Giulio Casserio of Padua,
Bought her for science, questioned her with his knife,
And drawn her for his great *Anatomy*;

Where still in the abundance of her grace,
She stands among the monuments of time
And with a feminine delicacy displays
His elegant dissection: the sublime
Shaft of her body opens like a flower
Whose petals, folded back expose the womb,
Cord and placenta and the sleeping child,
Like instruments of music in a room
Left when her grieving Orpheus left his tower
Forever, for the desert and the wild.

Naked she waits against a tideless shore,
A sibylline stance, a noble human frame
Such as those old anatomists loved to draw.
She turns her head as though in trouble or shame,
Yet with a dancer's gesture holds the fruit
Plucked, though not tasted, of the Fatal Tree.
Something of the first Eve is in this pose
And something of the second in the mute
Offering of her child in death to be
Love's victim and her flesh its mystic rose.

No figure with wings of fire and back-swept hair
Swoops with his: Blessed among Women!; no sword
Of the spirit cleaves or quickens her; yet there
She too was overshadowed by the Word,
Was chosen, and by her humble gift of death
The lowly and the poor in heart give tongue,
Wisdom puts down the mighty from their seat;
The vile rejoice and rising, hear beneath
Scalpel and forceps, tortured into song,
Her body utter their magnificat.

Four hundred years since first that cry rang out:
Four hundred years, the patient, probing knife
Cut towards its answer—yet we stand in doubt:
Living, we cannot tell the source of life.
Old science, old certainties that lit our way
Shrink to poor guesses, dwindle to a myth.
Today's truths teach us how we were beguiled;
Tomorrow's how blind our vision of today.
The universals we thought to conjure with
Pass: there remain the mother and the child.

Loadstone, loadstar, alike to each new age,
There at the crux of time they stand and scan,
Past every scrutiny of prophet or sage,
Still unguessed prospects in this venture of Man.
To generations, which we leave behind,
They taught a difficult, selfless skill: to show
The mask beyond the mask beyond the mask;
To ours another vista, where the mind
No longer asks for answers, but to know:
What questions are there which we fail to ask?

Who knows, but to the age to come they speak
Words that our own is still unapt to hear:
"These are the limits of all you sought and seek;
More our yet unborn nature cannot bear.
Learn now that all man's intellectual quest
Was but the stirrings of a foetal sleep;
The birth you cannot haste and cannot stay
Nears its appointed time; turn now and rest
Till that new nature ripens, till the deep
Dawns with that unimaginable day."

LOVING KIND

Loving Kind went by the way,
Hapless Loving Kind,
Up and down, by night and day,
Her true love to find.

Roving eye and nimble tongue
All her paths pursue:
How should she, and she so young,
Know false love from true?

Some by grace she would compel;
None would she deny:
How shall I my true love tell
Only passing by?

Sober heart and prudent mind
Scorn her and reprove:
How should she by loving find
Any truth in love?

Yet she smiled and smiling said:
Though my love I see
Except I take him to my bed,
How shall he know me?

THE APOTELESM OF W. B. YEATS

Such a grand story
Of Willy Yeats,
Keeping his warm bed
Under the slates
To a tale of milkmaids
His friend relates:

"At churns in Sligo
The wenches hum:
Come butter, Come butter,
Come butter,
Come!
Every lump as
Big as my bum!"

A milkmaid mounting
The poet's stair;
A blackbird trilling
His country air;
Butter and bottom,
The Muse was there.

Sheep in the meadow,
Cows in the corn;
Come Willy Butler
Blow up your horn!
Out of such moments
Beauty is born.

[Note: See the story in Oliver St John Gogarty's: *As I was Going Down Sackville Street*, pp. 115-117.]

TIGER

"At noon the paper tigers roar."—Miroslav Holub.

The paper tigers roar at noon;
The sun is hot, the sun is high.
They roar in chorus, not in tune,
Their plaintive, savage hunting cry.

O, when you hear them, stop your ears
And clench your lids and bite your tongue.
The harmless paper tiger bears
Strong fascination for the young.

His forest is the busy street;
His dens the forum and the mart;
He drinks no blood, he tastes no meat:
He riddles and corrupts the heart.

But when the dusk begins to creep
From tree to tree, from door to door,
The jungle tiger wakes from sleep
And utters his authentic roar.

It bursts the night and shakes the stars
Till one breaks blazing from the sky;
Then listen! If to meet it soars
Your heart's reverberating cry,

My child, then put aside your fear:
Unbar the door and walk outside!
The real tiger waits you there;
His golden eyes shall be your guide.

And, should he spare you in his wrath,
The world and all the worlds are yours;
And should he leap the jungle path
And clasp you with his bloody jaws,

Then say, as his divine embrace
Destroys the mortal parts of you:
I too am of that royal race
Who do what we are born to do.

ADVICE TO A POET

As you walk through the garden of this world,
Holding in your hands this crystal Now,
Passed down by Father Adam from son to son,
See on every bush the meanings furled
In tight unopening buds; then look and know
How in this glass they open one by one;

How as you tend your vines and plant and hoe,
These buds become your poems and fill the air
With longing, with madness. But, when the petals fall,
Thick on the bough the ripening apples grow
For somebody's wife who knows you set them there
As the recurring sacraments of her Fall.

Then show your age the discipline of that tree;
Show them the images common sense denied;
Teach them to hear the music of all they do;
Replant their garden of innocence; let them see
Beyond the markets of power, chimneys of pride,
Man in free fall, never quite knowing where to.

But never forget the garden, never forget
That's where he falls from, that's where he longs to return;
Always remember the launching site and the bride
Intoning his count-down: "Ready, get ready, get set,
GO!" As he blasts, he opens his orders to learn
Too late, the lady has taken him for a ride.

"Ah well, they are always looking for someone to launch,"
He reflects, and adds: "But that's what women are for;
Look at me now: I *thought* I was going to bed!"
The expendable sex, he opens his sandwich lunch,
Corrects his course dead on for the Evening Star
And grins as he taps out his message: "Trouble ahead!"

When she reads that out, someone is sure to laugh;
And that's where your job begins: the function of verse
Is to provide a carrier-wave for the soul's
Venture into the void; and the epitaph
Of the doomed explorers of the universe
Is the map you make from their log-books; between two poles

Called "I leave" and "I love", their ego-sounding devices
Probe her cloud-mantle, crying: "Is any one there?"
Their instruments crackle and spit in the cosmic wind.
Out of that white noise yours is the ear that prises
Signals which plotted in series show the bare
Body of Venus they came so far to find.

So tell them: they will not believe you; they will not even
Comprehend what you say about that planet.
They will jeer at the crystal you carry in your hands;
But tell them, tell them: their need to be forgiven
Will make them listen. Listen yourself for the minute
When tears break through as somebody understands.

But one thing you must not tell, though of course you know it,
Since all that we are hangs on this thought alone:
The word that we carry within us only for God.
What father Adam, the exile, the bare-arse poet,
Taught me, I teach to you: learn, practise and pass it on!
(Now read my lines again: this is a message in code.)

A VISIT TO THE RUINS

This charming archaeologist, with her spade,
Surveys my ruins, measures the daisied mound,
Three mouldering plinths, one column still erect.
Her twenty summers from its millennial shade
Take stock of all that history underground.
Cutting the first sods, what does she expect?

Has she some theory, or is she digging blind?
Does dream or sober fact impel her, while
She sinks a trial trench, pegs out her grid?
Is it foreknowledge of what she hopes to find
Moulds her young mouth to that archaic smile?
And when her spade rings on the marble lid,

The King's sarcophagus, all its seals intact,
Still smiling will she raise his golden mask,
Touch with warm lips that face of crumbling bone,
Or will its hollow sockets not refract
Tears dropping from live eyes again? I ask,
Will she disturb my quiet or her own?

Or, if she seeks inscriptions, to restore
From primitive script my long-lost Song of Songs,
Whose extant fragments baffle her scholar's art,
Has she the scholar's instinct, which before
She spells its words, by the true Gift of Tongues,
Can call their music already from her heart?

Thinking to reconstruct me as I was
In the great years before the Kingdom fell,
Can she imagine such arrogant splendour; can
Her notes from cinder, debris, sherds and dross
Bring to fierce life the tale these relics tell
Of those last moments when the sack began:

The throne-room wrecked, the roar of "kill and kill!",
The women raped and slaughtered where they lie,
The shattered images ravished of their gold,
And, whiter than his statue and as still,
The young King, dying in all that butchery,
Watching the hangings as the flames take hold?

Well, if she can! Some things her practised eye
Will miss: her sceptic mind will not observe
Ghosts slink to deeper layers among the dead;
She will not hear a skeleton's minimal sigh
Greet the sharp sun, nor, as she turns fresh turf,
The mandrake's shriek, torn bleeding from its bed.

No training could enable her to foresee
Her last discovery when it comes to pass:
The eponymous founder's tomb, identified,
Gapes as the granite slab is levered free;
She steps towards that black hole and sees, alas,
That there is nothing, nothing at all inside!

Nothing . . . and then the darkness swirls and sighs
And, out of the illimitable past,
A voice of terror, speaking her own tongue,
Calls her by name, and calls again, and cries:
"At last you have come home, at last, at last!
Where have you been, child, why did you stay so long?"

SONNETS TO BAUDELAIRE
For Norman Holmes Pearson

I

These thoughts which I return you are your due
Not so much that in origin most were yours,
As that of all those spirits who know what laws
Forge Irony to Beauty, it was you
Drank deepest of that pure sardonic draught;
You, naked, the first gardener under God,
Who tilled our rotting paradise, from its sod
Raised monstrous blooms and taught my tongue the craft.

For we are fellow travellers in a land
Where few around us know they walk in hell,
Where what they take for the creating Word
Is a blind wind sowing the sand with sand.
Brother, it is our task of love to tell
Men they are damned, and damned in being absurd.

II

Well, to begin, here's a nice tit for tat:
I like your note to old Pharaoh, Monselet,
How, from unspeakable Brussels, on your way
To Uccle—unpronounceable at that!—
You found yourself, on Belgium's dreary flat,
In a pub with a signboard, so you say:
"*A la Vue du Cimitière, Estaminet!*"
You've had your innings: It's my turn to bat!

In Lisbon, two years since, I took a tram
"*Cimiterio des Prazeres*" read its sign!
I thought of possible meanings all day, all
By-blows of Nature, who does not give a damn.
But, also in Lisbon she gave me her divine
Banco Espirito Sante e Commercial!

III

A Man of Letters, Hippolyte Babou,
—God help us, but there's *something* in a name!—
A Man of Taste, a Critic of some fame,
Misread your *Fleurs du Mal* but praised them too.
And J.-J. Weiss—alas, he never knew
B from a bull's foot—called them trite and tame,
Insipid and obscene. It seems a shame
Time should leave both to welter in the pooh!

But ah, to see great ruining Time set back
These self-appointed police of taste and style,
The pompous claims, the hollow judgments crack,
Ridicule shrivel that smug olympian calm,
Brings poets when we meet, once in a while,
What belly-laughs, what recompense, what balm!

IV

He warms my heart, your Monsieur Monselet;
—Such culture addicts, such genteel amateurs
As scold us for "abominable verse",
While, savage with joy, we let them have their say—

Poor fellow, I see him scan your lines, his eyes
Moist with fine feeling, till they meet the words
About the hanged man's belly ripped by birds:
"His dangling bowels dribbled down his thighs!"

"Ah, monstrous line!" You smile and shake your head:
"Monstrous, and perfect! What else could I do?
A poem is not a game; the image I chose
Was what my theme required. But what would you
—Put yourself in my place—have wished instead?"
And Monsieur Monselet replies: "A Rose!"

V

Here's News from Muscovy to delight us both:
Aseev, Khlebnikov, Mayakovsky and Co,
Those Futurists half a century ago
Cutting new coats regardless of their cloth.
"Throw Pushkin overboard," I quote them straight,
"From the great steamship of Modernity!
Cast Tolstoy, Dostoevsky to the sea!"
In nineteen twelve that sounded up-to-date.

They were poets, and not such bad ones. We may laugh
And say the Future was not theirs to read
And yet their image was exquisitely just,
Such emblems as become an epitaph:
That steamship, obsolete as the Futurist creed,
This heap of scrap; their sea, that bowl of dust.

VI

Having left Pushkin bleeding on the snow
George D'Anthès, dapper instrument of doom,
Sleek as a seal, purring like any tom,
Went back to France. Blood was his passport to
A railway fortune, a bank, a mission or so;
Three emperors rewarded his aplomb;
He had, to crown it all at last, become
President of the Paris Gaslight Co.

Did you rejoice to know, since now and then
Nature achieves what Art would hardly dare,
At nightfall, as you watched crepuscular
Demons swarm to work like business men,
Your wicked city, your Paris, *la ville lumière*,
Lit by the man who quenched the morning star?

VII

Why women should outlive men, the wits aver,
Is that the hazards that confront the human
Give men one more to face than women: Woman!
She is the earth: he digs his grave in her,
The insatiate sea that drowns the tallest mast,
The gorgon sky that stares his dreams to stone,
The mould that quietly eats him to the bone,
The long, long night in which he sleeps at last.

Was it your luck or genius to discover
That living is this voyage among the dead,
That poets have one task: to tell the brave
How all his victories must be lost in bed
And in the womb say to each unborn lover:
The hand that rocks the cradle rules the grave.

VIII

That was one view of Woman I cannot share.
The wound was self-inflicted, I recall,
You suffered, but was there any need at all
For all that martyrdom, horror and despair?
I think you did not fool yourself. You knew
Woman was your laboratory; your delight,
Stretched by that frightful female in the night,
Was a pure scientist's pleasure in the New.

Much worse of course, than your grand tour of Hell,
Are the ideals, the sisters of your choice,
Statues in sugar on their pedestals,
Your hymns *à l'ange, à l'idole immortelle*!
Thank God at times you heard the deep that calls
To the great deep, Love's unmistakable voice.

IX

The voyage we do not take to the unknown
Becomes the poem that visits us instead;
Its metaphor: two lovers in a bed
Lost to the flesh, exploring towards the bone.
Though one is underneath and one above,
They are one body, one motion and one breath,
Where each caress becomes an act of faith
And every simile an act of love.

Here you struck truth; here you divined a need
In every man, in every woman too
To bare the bone of their necessity,
Give all, hold nothing back, to break, to bleed.
Isolde does the thing she has to do
And drinks and casts the cup into the sea.

X

You saw it rise, I see it set, that sun,
The bright aubade, the serenade's dying fall,
Between us, brother, we have seen it all.
What was it worth, now all is said and done,
The great Romantic theme: *My heart laid bare?*
One thing, like Ozymandias, they forgot:
To make it worth the trouble, someone must care

To watch Narcissus give himself a hug
Or Onan practise on his magic flute.
Now as the stars light up, for better or worse
Time throws away the key that locked those smug
Museums of self-regard, the universe
Expands, but something's slimy underfoot.

XI

Your ancient, unknown author asks: What can
Match that man's joy who drinks the man-made wine,
Except a deeper ecstasy, the divine
Joy of the wine to feel itself made man?
Thus poets see Nature's temple, less a place
Of living pillars where all things correspond,
Than one where each world knows a world beyond
And all things yearn for that supreme embrace.

All things solicit the poet for his art
To change dumb being into sentient wine;
Flowers turn their faces, stones implore his feet.
Drunk with those lives, he reels towards the sign
Where, in his turn, the secular paraclete
Cries: Drink, engulf me, let me feel my heart.

XII

Crénom! your last word, as it could be mine,
(It shocked those pious sisters in the ward)
Speech, Poetry, the Holy Name, the Word,
Became a grunt, last human act and sign.
What of it? The butt-end of a harmless oath
Showed, like the glint of your still living eyes,
Not Life, not Death had taken you by surprise:
With love and irony you met them both.

Women you had loved stood smiling by your bed;
Crénom! you sighed: it was the last caress.
They played you Wagner and again a blurred
Crénom! came like an echo from the Dead.
Crénom! Name, number, the creating word
Utters the heart's unhesitating: Yes!

"WITH THEE CONVERSING..."

Talking with you each day would seem
To pass unnoticed into night,
And, borne on that enchanted stream,
Time but its pulse of dark and light;

And even busied or apart,
I feel the current's restless sweep:
A conversation fills the heart,
Or voices answer in my sleep.

Nor does it move by words alone:
Beneath our smiles, our talk, beneath
All words, a colloquy goes on
Which runs as strong and still as death.

Where did it rise, that mighty flow
On which, chance travellers, we embark?
What cordilleras feed with snow
Its cataracts raging through the dark,

I cannot guess, nor yet foresee
What hour the flood, as we descend,
Will turn and sweep us to the sea
In which all rivers have their end.

Talking with you, I cease to care
Where the springs rise and where they flow;
The goal of all my search is here
And here my everlasting Now.

SIX SONGS FOR CHLOË

I

The Vintage

The grapes that in my vineyard grow
Ripen and load the heavy boughs.
I cut the clustering fruit and go
Laden myself toward the house
To heap them on my table there
And sit and watch them from my chair.

Exquisite in their grace and bloom,
Their perfect ripeness, fragrance, youth,
With invitation fill the room
And they implore the poet's mouth
To ravish, to bite deep, to taste
And make them one with him at last.

But no, the poet smiles to see
Their urgent, innocent distress:
He takes them in their ecstasy,
Tumbles them in his cruel press
And, while the must runs strong and sweet,
Tramples them with his bloody feet,

Then pours their blood into his vats
And there ferments them into song
In which transmuted beauty waits
Her last perfection ages long
For men unborn to taste and praise
The masterwork of ancient days.

But when my wine is laid in store,
I come home weary and athirst
And sit and for myself I pour
A wine of ageless beauty first
And till it glows in heart and head,
Chloë, I shall not come to bed;

For, while my eyes delight to view
That lustrous, fresh, delicious shape,
The great debate my thoughts renew
Between the liquor and the grape,
And, while I know you hate the thought,
Love blesses me with double sport;

Though in your arms at lover's work
All night I labour and rejoice,
My soul reviews like any Turk
The vintages it has at choice
And all your charms I then rehearse
And plan to bottle you in verse.

II

The Perfume

". . . marked males of the silkworm moth have been known to fly upwind seven miles to a fragrant female of their kind . . . the chemical compound with which a female silkworm moth attracts mates is highly specific; no other species seem aware of it. In 1959, the Nobel Laureate Adolph Butenandt of the Max Planck Institute for Bio-chemistry in Munich succeeded in analysing it. He found it to be an alcohol with sixteen carbon atoms per molecule. . . ."

[L. and M. Milne: *The Senses of Animals and Men*.]

O Chloë, have you heard it,
   This news I sing to you?
It's true, my lovely bird, it
   Is absolutely true!
A biochemist probing
   Has caught without a doubt
The Queen of Love disrobing
   And found her secret out.

What drives the *Bombyx mori*
   To fly, intrepid male,
Lured by the old, old story
   Six miles against the gale?
The formula, my Honey,
   Is now in print to prove
What is, and no baloney,
   The very stuff of love.

At Munich on the Isar
   Those molecules were found
Which everyone agrees are
   What makes the world go round;

What draws the male creation
  To love, my darling doll,
Turns out, on trituration,
  To be an alcohol.

A Nobel Laureatus
  Called Adolph Butenandt
Contrived to isolate us
  This strong intoxicant.
The boys are celebrating
  And singing at the club:
Here's Bottoms up! to mating,
  Since Venus keeps a pub!

My angel, O, my angel,
  What is it *you* suffuse,
What redolent evangel,
  What nosegay of good news?
What draws me like a dragnet
  And holds and keeps me tight?
What odds! my fragrant magnet,
  I shall be drunk tonight!

III

Going to Bed

Chloë, let down that chestnut hair;
Let it flow full; let it fall free;
Loosen that zone, those clasps that bare
Your breasts: then leave the rest to me.

First like a cloud your dress shall float
Over your shoulders and away;
And next the faithless petticoat
Those exquisite, breathing flanks display;

Stockings and drawers I shall peel off
From your lithe legs and lovely thighs,
And think the rustling silks you slough
The foam from which, new-born, you rise.

Thus Love in mime despoils this world:
Fashions, beliefs and customs fall;
In brutal, naked grace unfurled
He shows the root and ground of all.

But when his power has stripped us stark,
These purged and primal selves shall find
A better and a brighter mark
Than those poor ventures of mankind;

For we whose fate is to retrace
The labyrinth and re-wind the clew,
All patterns of the past erase
And find our world begins anew.

Our nature then puts off, my dear,
What parts it from the true divine:
Bare as the gods we must appear
And as those blessed beings shine.

A single, soaring flame shall bound,
Frame and enfold our nakedness;
And with that glory clothed and crowned
Our souls shall want no other dress.

No roof can shelter us, no house
That falls to ruin as fabrics must;
No crumbling temple hear our vows
Or sanction that immortal lust.

Our bed must be the bracken brown
Or the waste dunes beside the sea,
And the wide heaven arching down
Our portion of eternity.

IV

The Quarrel

Chloë, be still!
Not one word more;
The gale is not so shrill
Under my door.

Shriek, then, fury, shriek:
Call me brute and worse!
Where was I this week?
I was writing verse.

Do you doubt me then?
Have you sworn to prove
That I spent it in
Bed making love?

Who then, who, hell-cat?
Only tell her name.
What, you dare say that:
Chloë, hush, for shame!

Never think a few
Tears will soften me.
I've a mind to lay you
Across my knee.

What was that, you vixen,
Words I hear you spit?
"You and who else then?"
Let me show you, pet.

See, I've got you, precious,
Skirt folded back
To give that delicious
Bottom one smack.

One more, permit me!—
Then another one—
—Hell, girl you bit me
Almost to the bone!

Girls should be made of
Sugar and spice;
Girls should be afraid of
Brutal men and mice.

But not my Chloë; she's
A brimstone wench;
Dragon, cockatrice
Would not make her blench.

Chloë, what is this?
After lightning, rain?
Do you sob and kiss,
Are you mild again?

Do you hate me less?
Do you nod your head?
Yes, Yes, Yes!
Chloë, come to bed!

V

The Lamp

Night and the sea; the firelight glowing;
We sit in silence by the hearth;
I musing, you beside me sewing,
We glean the long day's aftermath.

After the romping surf, the laughter,
The salt and sun, the roaring beach,
These flames glancing on wall and rafter
Are tongues of pentecostal speech.

And while their whispers come and go, I
Turn to watch you in your grace,
My gallant, radiant, reckless Chloë,
Who love and lead me such a chase,

To find it vanished, that incessant
Fulfilment of the urgent Now:
For here, absolved from past and present,
There broods a girl I do not know.

The clear, the gay, the brilliant nature
Matching your body's pride, gives place
To a soft, wavering change of feature:
This grave, remote and troubled face;

A face all women have in common
When, lost within themselves, alone,
They hear the demiourgos summon
And draw their ocean like the moon.

The moon is up; the beaches glisten,
The land grows faceless as the sea;
And you withdraw and, while you listen,
Put on your anonymity.

I hear my pulses, as they travel,
Drop one by one to the abyss;
I feel the skein of life unravel
And ask in dread: who then is this?

Who is this shade that sits beside me
And on what errand has she come:
To drive me on the dark, or guide me,
To tempt, or bring my spirit home?

Or is she lost herself, uncertain
And helpless on that timeless track?
Whichever way, I draw the curtain
And light the lamp that brings us back.

VI

The Lunch

Under these trellised vines, below
The summer trees our table waits;
A smiling waiter lays our plates.
Ah, Chloë, will you leave me now?
For though you may come back, you say,
How shall I live until that day?

Shall we have oysters on the shell?
Shall we choose mushrooms with the steak?
I never thought a heart could break
Between two sips of the moselle:
You laugh and ask me if my heart
Breaks *table d'hôte* or *à la carte*.

Laugh, Chloë, that delightful sound
Restores my spirits with my sense.
The present is the only tense
For love to make the world go round
And round and round until the sea
That takes you, bears you back to me.

Laugh, Chloë; in an hour you sail.
Let us remember while we can:
You are a woman, I a man
And nothing those two words entail
Of ventured or unbidden joy
Can time deny us or destroy.

Do you you recall how long ago
You taught me with a laughing glance
To set my heart upon the dance
And let the dancers come and go
Since the fulfilment of desire
Asks still to feed, not fix, that fire?

Look up: the grapes are on the vine,
Green promises, unripe as yet;
Only two summers since we met
And just a year you have been mine,
Yet in that brief eternity
You have remade the world and me.

But when I try to keep it so
You look and laugh and raise your glass
And answer: "Only things that pass
Live and renew themselves and grow;
A love that does not change is dead
And offers stone for living bread.

"These oysters smelling of the brine
Are now our summer by the sea;
Those grapes, though sour still, will be
Next summer's heritage of wine;
Love's every landfall is one more
Departure for an unknown shore.

"You will not be, suppose we meet
Next year, the man you are today,
Nor I the girl who went away;
And if we never do, my sweet,
You may promote this changing heart
To be a changeless work of art.

"For whether I come back or no,
You are a poet, I a theme
Composed to realize your dream.
I was content to have it so,
Since I too have my art: to give
Visions the flesh by which they live.

"But this is done: who would repeat
One rôle to the last tick of time?
Break off now at the peak and prime,
Not at love's wane or its retreat
To which all natures in the end
Come if they live at all, my friend.

"You fight against it still? Recall:
Your first song set me by to be
A vintage for futurity,
A part no woman likes at all.
And now your wine is poured, I think:
Like it or not, but you must drink."

Yes, Chloë, so I said at first
When I, as the magician then
Transformed you with my magic pen;
But now the parts are quite reversed:
Only your power supplanting mine
Can change my water into wine.

And yet each power in turn has made
This love which is both life and art
Where each of us has played our part
Of mutual and essential aid
By which the weak soul comes to be
Capable of eternity.

Now it is done: that noble draught
Is poured for me. I shall not shrink
And as a toast to you I drink!
For, the first time we met you laughed,
And, Chloë, you are laughing still.
Here comes the waiter with my bill.

THE SCHOOL OF NIGHT

What did I study in your School of Night?
When your mouth's first unfathomable yes
Opened your body to be my book, I read
My answers there and learned the spell aright,
Yet, though I searched and searched, could never guess
What spirits it raised nor where their questions led.

Those others, familiar tenants of your sleep,
The whisperers, the grave somnambulists
Whose eyes turn in to scrutinize their woe,
The giant who broods above the nightmare steep,
That sleeping girl, shuddering, with clenched fists,
A vampire baby suckling at her toe,

They taught me most. The scholar held his pen
And watched his blood drip thickly on the page
To form a text in unknown characters
Which, as I scanned them, changed and changed again:
The lines grew bars, the bars a Delphic cage
And I the captive of his magic verse.

But then I woke and naked in my bed
The words made flesh slept, head upon my breast;
The bed rode down the darkness like a stream;
Stars I had never seen danced overhead.
"A blind man's fingers read love's body best:
Read all of me!" you murmured in your dream.

"Read me, my darling, translate me to your tongue,
That strange Man-language which you know by heart;
Set my words to your music as they fall;

Soon, soon, my love! The night will not be long;
With dawn the images of sleep depart
And its dark wisdom fades beyond recall."

Here I stand groping about the shores of light
Too dazzled to read that fading palimpsest;
Faint as whisper that archaic hand
Recalls some echo from your school of night
And dead sea scrolls that were my heart attest
How once I visited your holy land.

LIEDER OHNE BUCHSTABEN

Each poet builds in verse
For every age to see:
His monument, a brass
    Eternity.

I would not have it so,
No towers, no tombs, no shows.
As a bird to the green bough
    Love comes, love goes.

I call no witnesses;
The songs I make for you
Should pass like a caress
    Or the bright dew,

The assent of meeting eyes
When rapture, when laughter
Take silence by surprise;
    And silence after;

World in parenthesis,
Smiles we exchange,
Momentary as this kiss;
    As fierce, as strange.

Such songs I would prepare
As for our supper spread,
Songs we as simply share
    As wine and bread;

Songs for each place and mood,
All seasons of the heart,
And one for solitude
    When we two part.

Then to make one song more:
A song the bird alone
Sings after as before
    His love has flown.

He sings his first song still
Although his heart is wrung,
For love may change at will,
    But not his song.

WHEN LIKE THE SUN . . .

When like the sun I warm her snow,
She smiles above and melts below
And my caress between her thighs
Revives the dew of paradise.

Those glands of Bartholin I bless,
The sweet wild honey they express,
The exquisite faint scent they bring
Of mountain flowers in early spring.

O, let me be your bee and rove
The heaths and tufted slopes of love,
Gather that honey all day long
And breathe its fragrance in my song.

AS WELL AS THEY CAN

As well as it can, the hooked fish while it dies,
Gasping for life, threshing in terror and pain,
Its torn mouth parched, grit in its delicate eyes,
    Thinks of its pool again.

As well as he can, the poet, blind, betrayed
Distracted by the groaning mill, among
The jostle of slaves, the clatter, the lash of trade,
    Taps the pure source of song.

As well as I can, my heart in this bleak air,
The empty days, the waste nights since you went,
Recalls your warmth, your smile, the grace and stir
    That were its element.

THE GREAT BABOONS

I am the last King of the Great Baboons
Who are all dead now, every one but me,
My people, a good people, brave and strong.
I was their king and, as I taught them, they
Worshipped Old Hairy, the Baboon Supreme
Who lives above the sky and only speaks
When he is angry. When they heard his voice,
They would be still and listen and leave off
Fighting or mating, browsing, picking fleas
And watch me as I barked back from this rock;
And sometimes they would ask me what he said.

My people, a good people, but not wise:
They fought, they fed, they mated and they slept;
I ruled them and I taught them to be strong.
Even the lions feared them in their rage
When, manes a-bristle and great canines bared,
My foragers charged and drove them from a kill.
And, at the first, content with what they had;
Their test of most things: is it good to eat?
Great quarrellers, it kept them quick and keen;
Great maters, they were at it day and night;
And when they slept, I was their sentinel,
Sitting alone up here beneath the stars.

Those were the times Old Hairy talked to me;
We would consult each other as king to king;
Sometimes I asked him what was best to do;
Sometimes he grumbled, sometimes told me tales
Of the old fathers, the first Great Baboons
And once he asked me what they thought of him,
The people he had given into my care.

"Well, Hairy," I answered, "it is hard to tell.
They say they worship you, and yet I know
The only things they think about are four:
Fuck, fight, food, fleas; you know, the four great F's
Old Hairy gave baboons to think about.
What *they* call thinking's quite another thing:
In the new moon, when all baboons are wild,
They meet for 'think-think' in the great ravine.
They have a language for it, full of words,
Delicious words that make them drunk with joy.
'Love', they say, 'love'; baboons were made for love.
'Duty', they say, 'Art', 'Philosophy',
'Science' and 'Culture'; God knows what beside;
I listen just as little as I can;
A king can't be mixed up in things like that.
A king must rule and keep his common sense
And hold the peace those words would soon destroy.
You know this, Hairy, you a king like me.

"I tell my people of you when they ask:
You made the world, a good baboon-made world,
And best of all your works you made baboons.
Each night you turn the mountains up like stones
And find delicious grubs there five miles long;
When a star falls, I point to it and say:
'Old Hairy plucking berries from the sky!
He makes a long arm, children, so beware!'
Sometimes at twilight sitting here I see
A female coming from the water-hole,
Her tail a-wagging in a special way,
And when the others gather round she tells
How someone seized her as she stooped to drink,
Someone behind her whom she did not see:
'Prodigious mating and prodigious joy!

A hundred times he mounted me and spent;
Yet, when I turned to flea him, he was gone.
'That must have been Old Hairy,' I reply.
And true enough, their young are sure to grow
To giant baboons, almost as huge as me,
Warriors and mates to whom all things give way.

"Then when they hear your anger's rumbling growl
Roll round the sky and see it split with fire
That makes the valleys shake and brings the rain,
They squat up close and ask me what you mean,
Believing you have special words like theirs,
The 'think-think' words they use in the ravine.
I tell them, no! I tell them how at night
Keeping my watch, their king, their sentinel,
Sitting with you, and talking, king with king,
I feel your fingers prowling through my fur
And hear your teeth crack on celestial fleas.
They know this, but my people are not wise;
They mix you up with those mad words of theirs."

Old Hairy laughed: a great slice of the cliff
Sheered off and crashed to the ravine below.
Old Hairy laughed and tugged my royal mane.
"The tree, tell them about the tree," he growled,
"Seven days, seven nights toward the east it grows,
Always in fruit, great golden fruit that hang
Thick on the boughs, juicy and sweet and strong.
Till now it was forbidden my baboons,
Last made of all things when I made the world,
But now the time has come for them to know
Good customs from the evil that destroy.

"Tomorrow early, walk towards the sun
Seven days, seven nights, and I will be your guide,
And find the tree and break yourself a bough
And bear it back to make your people wise."

The sun rose. I set off. I found the tree,
Tasted the fruit; it made me drunk with joy;
Tore off a branch, came singing, reeling back
Seven days, seven nights and reached my people's caves
And called them to me: there was no reply.
They were all gone. I called and searched and called.
I sat and waited: none of them came back.
And when at last I found them, they were dead.
No, one still breathed and just before he died
He told me what had happened.

                        Left alone,
My foolish people, left without their king,
Went wild. When I had left them seven nights
The new moon rose. From then till my return
They held a "think-think" in Old Hairy's name.
Each night they made up new and headier words
Which drove them to a frenzy; every day
They used them in wild arguments to prove
That some baboons are right and some are wrong.
My poor baboon was dying—a broken back—
He could not well remember all those words;
But on the fifth day, so he said, they made
In Hairy's name, such words as "sin" and "soul",
"Salvation", "conscience" and "immortal life";
And the strong poison drove them all apart
To hate each other by so-called "moral law".
Such nonsense! but for the first time it was
Baboons against baboons in parties, not,
As it should be, baboons against the world.

On the sixth night they found new words again:
"Liberty", "justice", "brotherhood of baboons",
"Enlightenment", "The Social Contract"—well,
I ask you! As the great debate went on
It was decided I must be deposed:
No kings, no kings, since all baboons are free.
But on the seventh a new quarrel broke out
On what was the best state for all baboons
To live in, now that kings had ceased to rule.
Two of the "Sons of Hairy", as we call
Baboons begotten at the water-hole,
Took issue: they were eloquent and strong.
Soon force or fear or foolishness of words
Brought half my people to each side. At first
Two parties, then two armies, then two mobs
Maddened to fight, to kill, to tear to shreds
Their brothers in the name of brotherhood,
Even the breeding females, even the babes
In arms all creatures spare, they tore apart.

I had forgotten Old Hairy. The first night
Of the new moon he thought it would be sport
To hear a "think-think"; so, with me away,
He came and sat here on the king's own rock.
Night after night he came and heard it all,
All that insane corroboree of words.
All night he listened but left before the dawn.
He watched, but what he thought nobody knew.
Not one of all my word-crazed children saw
That mighty shadow blotting out the stars.
But on the seventh night, the massacre
Of brothers in the cause of brotherhood,
When all were bloody and half of them were dead
He stirred. Then suddenly Old Hairy laughed

And as before, a great piece of the cliff
Fell ruining down and finished all the rest.
Next morning just at sunrise I came back
Bringing my people the once-forbidden fruit
But found them gone: the fruit had come too late.

Now they are all dead. Here among the rocks
With only Him to talk to, it is sad.
I mourn my foolish people and I yearn
For the good talk I had with them before
And that good life based in the four great F's.
Old Hairy, too, is changed: he never speaks
A language now that I can understand.
I lost his tongue that time I ate the fruit
And when I speak to him, he sometimes keeps
His answer back for hours, for days on end.
Only at midnight, drowsing here alone
Above these caves that need no sentinel,
An old mad king with nobody to rule,
I sense a shadow fall across my rock
And feel Old Hairy's fingers groom my scalp.

VIVALDI, BIRD AND ANGEL

or

IL CARDELLINO

For Diana

Indem sie über den Don Juan, über ihre Rolle sprach, war es, als öffneten sich mir nun erst die Tiefen des Meisterwerks, und ich konnte hell hineinblicken und einer fremden Welt phantastische Erscheinungen deutlich erkennen. Sie sagte, ihr ganzes Leben sei Musik, und oft glaube sie manches im Innern geheimnisvoll Verschlossene, was keine Worte aussprächen, singend zu begreifen.

[Hoffmann: *Don Juan, Eine Fabelhafte Begebenheit.*]

I. THE POET

A life that moves to music cannot fail
And a real music moves my fictive tale.
Vivaldi's goldfinch gave me my idea
And Canaletto's Venice the place; the year
(A guess) is seventeen twenty seven or eight;
The scene, imaginary, like the date,
Is furnished with a bird, a flowering tree
In the walled garden of a nunnery,
An angel, poised in air, who views the bird,
And both can see unseen and hear unheard
Through a great window of the *Pietà*,
Europe's best school of music, where there are
Grouped in spring sunlight round a cembalo
Five girls in scarlet habits with fiddle and bow.
A seated nun behind them, old and grave,
The chorus mistress, sees that they behave.
Chosen from foundlings the Venetian state
Takes in to nurture, rear, and educate,

Figlie del coro, their ages range between
A budding twelve, a radiant eighteen;
Bright eyed as birds, as lively and as shrill,
Daughters of Venice as one sees them still
In Longhi's paintings and Goldoni's plays.

But there is one girl more on whom the gaze
Rests with that sense of wonder and unease
Which perfect beauty imposes on the heart;
Holding a flute she stands a little apart
As fits a soloist who has won the right
Of *privilegiata*.   Here the light
Holds the fine planes and hollows of her cheeks
And her whole body listens while he speaks,
The chorus master, pointing to her score.
Nineteen years old, perhaps a little more,
She looks in slender strength and fine-drawn grace
A young Diana, breathing from the chase
And with that noble brow and eloquent eye,
The high small breasts, long flank and tapering thigh,
Among these plump, full-bosomed Venetians, she
Seems of a rarer breed and pedigree,
A falcon among doves, the formal pride
And challenge of an orchid set beside
Some cheerful vase of pinks or marigolds.
Now as the master speaks, she nods and holds
The flute against her mouth and tries a phrase.
That ripple of liquid notes has just the grace
Of her own motions, shoulder, neck and arm;
A gust that sweeps the corn from calm to calm
Gives just that sense of effortless ease and skill.
Her eyes question the master, grave and still;
He listens, smiles; she turns away released.

Antonio Vivaldi, the Red Priest,
Though the once flaming hair is ashen now,
Begins next to rehearse the cembalo.
Past fifty, though less old than he appears,
He has lived music all those fifty years.
His father, the first violinist of his day,
Gave him three crafts: to teach, compose and play;
But, though he is acknowledged in all three
The foremost master in all Italy,
A restless spirit, a contemplative mind
Take him beyond his age, to look behind
The mirror of art for that first cause which flies
Man's deepest and most passionate surmise.
And since a still-recurring weakness has
Meant he could never celebrate the mass,
His priesthood has been music: it is said
He consecrates its forms like wine and bread
And turns to this perpetual sacrifice
The service of the altar God denies.
Well that's as may-be: no man knows the heart
But there's a miracle in this great art,
A transubstantiation, a profound
And terrible joy to which the physical sound
Is but the body, the outward mould, the dress.

Today we see him in his happiness
Rehearsing his six pupils in a score
Of his composing, something never before
Tried, he believes, in music; soon to be
Pattern for the concerto and the key
To a whole pattern of music in our age.
He smiles, leafing the score to the last page,
Sits at the keyboard and begins to play
The bird theme, improvising by the way.

And, as the simple melody swells and grows
A sudden nimbus round the angel glows,
The bird stirs on its nest and all the air
Trembles as though the Spirit descended there
And made this room and garden holy ground.
And now he pauses: as the last notes sound
The moment passes and he takes his place
To start rehearsing for the thorough-bass.

Such are my actors: all will speak but one;
And though she cannot speak, she is the sun
Round which their questions all revolve, and she
Is both their answer and the mystery.
But as for two of them, I must give to each
The attributes of human thought and speech,
Give bird and angel minds which correspond
To ours because I cannot go beyond
My human limits. I let the music state
In its own terms what I, at best, translate.
Yes, trust the music: it completes my task;
Judge it by that. And, last, should someone ask:
Why have I chosen this point in time? Because
Somewhere beyond this frame of natural laws,
Moving in time on its predestined grooves,
I hear another music to which it moves.
Wherever I go, whatever I do, I seem
To step in time to that resistless stream
And though, I trust, a rational man, I vow
I heard it as a child, I hear it now;
With every year I live, it sounds more clear,
More vast, more jubilant to the inward ear;
Beyond my power to imagine or invent
That choir of being, or this sole instrument
Of my response to that invisible world.

Gift? or delusion? or defect unfurled
From genes that I inherit? I cannot tell;
I only know I hear it and, as well
That when I hear them humbly, as I do,
I know with pride, the masters heard it too.

II. THE BIRD

So clumsy, so gross, so awkward and so slow,
For hours they lurch and straddle to and fro,
For hours they grunt and splutter, I watch them there
Dull grovellers at the bottom of the air;
Yet, pointless, aimless creatures though they seem,
They live, they may be happy; perhaps they dream
And the dream helps them live, however absurd,
A swift, bright, effortless dream of being a bird!
It seems absurd indeed, and yet they do
Make love, defend their territories, build nests too,
And sometimes, as they are doing now, appear
To make long sequences pleasing to the ear
Even of birds, though meaningless enough,
Song, but a song I can make nothing of.
What are they doing there in that dark den?
Some mating ritual natural to men,
Such as birds practise, song, pursuit, display?
Yes, there it comes again, those curious, gay,
Disturbing sequences. . . .
                    Why there . . . and there . . .
It touched, it caught it . . . I could almost swear
It was indeed our mating song. . . .
                              Ah, no
It could not be . . . so clumsy, gross and slow
How could they . . . yet I wonder . . . there again!

So different, such strange joy . . . could things like men
Know rapture? Sing as birds will sometimes sing
For sheer delight? . . .
                         or even, my thoughts, taking wing;
I lose them . . . could they have some kind of song
Beyond my thought? I cannot tell . . . I . . . .

III. THE COMPOSER

So much for the continuo. As for the flute,
You, my dear Julia, must be absolute
For this performance, all depends on this,
Your reputation, and mine perhaps: it is
My bird concerto, *Il Cardellino*. See,
There she is peeping at us from that tree,
My little musician with the crimson mask,
Warming her five pale eggs. She does not ask
To go beyond her nature, but I do
Because I ask it even more of you.
God gave you beauty, a woman's shape and mind,
But not the voice; our *ospealiere* find
Fine husbands if they can sing pure and true;
God, who is just, denies that gift to you.
Ask, why should that be just? Perhaps it is
To strengthen some other, higher gift of his:
Yours is a genius for the flute, a rare
Skill for your age, a tone beyond compare,
And music in your very bones. . . . Well, well,
You know I do not flatter. Now I shall tell
You just what hard perfections I require:
You have the exquisite tact, the joy, the fire;
All I have asked, you mastered as I spoke;
Each time you played, new grace, new strength awoke;

Yet I need more from you: that perfect thing
Which makes the frame of being respond and sing,
Which goes beyond all effort, wit, intent:
The body united with the instrument.
The soul so deep in the composer's thought
That from the heart, inevitable, unsought
It plays itself—and then beyond the score
Beyond the players, another voice, a third
Presence, a new intelligence is heard.
But this you know already; you smile; I see
You recognize that sign, the mystery
By which each artist knows himself....
                                        Well now,
My bird concerto: the goldfinch, as you know,
Gave me my clue. The flute must catch the clear,
Pure goldfinch note throughout and yet, my dear,
You must not play it as though you were a bird
For that would make my whole design absurd,
No musical trifle, no imitations of
Brooks, birds, such as our light Venetians love.
No, I have tried, imagine if you can,
How a bird might compose it, if a man
Shared the bird nature; yes, and something more:
A bird that had an angel's heart might soar
Into an ecstasy past man's reach which still
Might lie within the grasp of human skill.
If you, my dear *maestra*, were that bird
So you would play and so it should be heard:
Bird's innocent rapture and man's pure technique,
Out of your angel's heart the flute must speak,
And all as of one nature.
                            Now at last
Try the whole consort. Keep that clear contrast
Of solo part with cembalo and strings.

Our *cognoscenti* who despise new things
Will pull sour faces, neither shuffle nor cough
Unless your very brilliance brings it off;
But if we triumph, it is a victory
Which may set instrumental music free,
Strike off the chains of our Andromeda
And finish in Venice what our morning star,
Fra Monteverdi with his magic bow
Began here round a hundred years ago.
He loosed sonata, to cantata tied:
I, in my turn, perhaps the first, have tried
To break the consort's interwoven flight.
One instrument, the flute, in its own right
Now speaks and leads the dance and, like a queen,
Commands and rules. You see here what I mean:
Here all is for the flute, even the key,
Re maggiore, I chose for her, for she
Avoids so those cross-fingerings which entail
Poor tone and in low notes may outright fail.

I have rested. Come now! Let us try once more!
Strings ready? Hand me here the master score!
Cembalo? So, so . . . Julia, give the note!
Take this first *tempo*, now, as though the throat
Of one rejoicing creature poured out all,
One angel heart, one bird voice, yet recall
The flute must lead in every note you play.
So now, *allegro*, one! two! and away.

Ah, God in heaven, they have it, it is done,
The lift, the ecstasy, the brilliant tone. . . .
My lovely Julia, that rapt face of hers,
That tone! . . . See, on her nest the goldfinch stirs
At the first trilling bird-call . . . ah, those trills,

What spirit, what ease! . . .
                       so effortless, yet it fills
All space and makes of time a living thing,
Soars like the bird itself. . . . Look at her now,
This exquisite child, that line of jaw and brow,
That faint flush coming and going against the white,
Those eloquent fingers, creatures in their own right
Dancing upon the dark shaft of the flute;
So unlike these other foundlings, common fruit
Of all too common beds, adulterous sheets,
Rapes, brothels, drunken nights and carnival streets;
No not their kind! She has the stamp of one
Got in the noble bed of Solomon
To Sheba's royal breed. . . . I miss my way
In thoughts like these. . . .
                       Enough, girls! Well, you play
Like angels as I hoped. Remember now:
This second *tempo, cantabile*, let it flow
With the pure singing tone, sustained and clear;
As though remote, contemplative you hear
The incantatory, grave voice of Spring.
Continuo? . . . Julia? . . . ready? Now let it sing.

They have it, they have it, it comes sweet and true
—Ah, but the flute, no! No, that will not do.
Stop there again! . . . Now Julia, for the tone:
Exquisite, rich, the crystal, the bared bone
Of melody white on Time's deserted shore!
But time! the time, my child! It should have more
Free, breathing ease. You would not have them say
We use in Venice, as someone surely may
Hearing this tap, tap, tap of even feet,
One of these new French pendulums for our beat,
Not Nature's, no, not our Venetian test!

For us Zacconi said it first, and best:
"The pulse of the heart is our true measure of time."
Let that pulse guide you: here a little climb,
There fall behind a little, as does the heart
Responsive to the moment, so in art.
Note puntate!—Look, child! Here's your score:
What did you think my dotted notes were for?
Now try it from the beginning without a break!

She has it now: there will be no mistake.
Now I may sit and listen and hear them through,
As God in Eden saw his work and knew
It good and took his pleasure in that sight.
Yet we musicians, perhaps, have more delight
Even than He: He saw the world he made;
We first review our works, then hear them played,
And I by his creation am doubly blest
In this child's beauty, crowning all the rest,
A beauty so like music . . . well, who knows?
Sometimes when I am settled to compose,
At night, beside my window, when the moon
Frets bright arpeggios over our lagoon,
The shining city, the mist, the sliding stars,
I hear, behind my score, the opening bars
Of a great harmony, tremendous tides
Of sound in which the whole creation rides.
Once while I knelt to hear them sing a mass
Of my composing, I knew for sure what was
That langauge which they spoke in Paradise:
Not Hebrew as some scholars still surmise,
But music. All their thought was melody,
Love a duet echoed from tree to tree;
The morning stars together began the day
Singing; all creatures sang at work or play;

From earliest dawn to latest afternoon
Each knew his part and none fell out of tune.
Then, as the twilight crept from hill to hill,
God walked among them and the air was still;
And in that solemn hush His voice was heard
Utter those primal chords which are the Word,
And as its resonant sweetness rolled and rang,
Untutored Adam raised his voice and sang.
The Snake, the Woman, the apple brought us this
Rabble of sound, clatter of grunt and hiss,
Which we call language; Babel made it worse.

Well, girls, you do well: you turn back the curse
Eve brought us. Think, on you the onus lies
To bring us back the tongue of Paradise!

IV. THE ANGEL

All creatures seek their food, and ours is song:
Each bodiless intelligence all day long
Both takes and proffers this transcendant cheer;
Yet when we range abroad beyond our sphere
On errands through this world of time and space,
Sometimes the burning messenger of grace
Will pause to hear a bird upon the wing,
A shepherd pipe, girls dancing in a ring,
Much as a prince who feasts at home each day,
Might stop to pick wild berries by the way.
I stopped to hear this bird; I stayed to hear
This concert: music for the physical ear,
Though crude beside those harmonies that fill
And move the universe, is music still
And in that mightier consort has some share.
It moves in every creature unaware;

All being is music, as Pythagoras thought;
But he, being only man, had scarcely caught
What that implies: that there are beings in time
As bodies in space. An angel in that prime
World of pure intellect, may move in space
Yet fills none, though for men to see his face
He must take visible shape. The eddy and swill
Of airy particles his creative will
Transforms to a bright plasma; in the grains
Of this rare state of matter, his spirit maintains
A body in space, where each related part
Subsists together, ruled by mind and heart,
A body in space because humanity
Cannot conceive of beings they cannot see.
But men born blind might easily defy
This slavery to the concepts of the eye,
And then I could as easily from air
Compel its molecules otherwise, appear
And take a body of sound, a being in time.
Such beings in their species match and rhyme
With those in space: each has inanimate
And living forms: the airs these girls create
Are not self-moved but, like their instruments,
Structures composed from lifeless elements
For all their intricate rational design;
Their minds like this intelligence of mine,
Are living beings and as the melodies grow
From flute and violins and cembalo
The living bodies sustain their spirits here,
Though it is otherwise in our timeless sphere.
Men, not being angels, do not know these things,
As though they knew the bird but not its wings
That give it flight, the throat but not the song.

Yet angels, though pure intellects, may go wrong:
A paradox of their natures is to know
The mind of God because he wills it so,
Yet not to read the minds and hearts of men,
Lower beings than we, and yet beyond our ken.
The music of this bird that sings for love
Is something, too, we have more inkling of
Than this rich harmony of strings and flute:
The one a means, the other an absolute;
The one all instinct shared from heart to heart,
The other's sole end and purpose: itself as art,
A blind and questing eloquence which flows
Not conscious whence it came or where it goes.
Since God has means beyond an angel's powers
This human art is still a riddle to ours;
For we, in the Great Music all immersed
Think it our nature and purpose last as first,
Where all compose, all know their parts and all
Contribute unbidden to that festival
Which is the dance of being, the universe.
There no one needs to learn, comply, rehearse.
So man is the exception, only man;
And yet we know, he too is in God's plan.
There's something in the human hid from us:
His solitude: no angel need discuss
Question or argue, disagree or brood:
All share with all. Man in his solitude
Creates, as though in ignorance of the real
Great Music by which angels think and feel
And feeling take their part without dissent.
Is it what God himself cannot prevent:
Natures which to be free must be apart,
Separate, inscrutable in mind and heart,

Wrestling alone with doubtful good and ill,
Where spirits, consenting in a higher will
Untroubled, by force of their consent are free?

Music for this bird in the flowering tree
Is pure communication, or almost so:
By song he calls his love or warns his foe,
And, if song gives them pleasure, like their gay
Colours, it is the enchantment of display.
Their exquisite language has some counterpart
In our great music which is neither art
Nor, in a sense, do we communicate
One with another in that perfect state;
Each knows the whole and by his part each finds
Total participation of lucid minds.
Unlike the music of men, our symphony
Is a great animate being, self-moving, free,
A living eloquence, a spiritual sun
Where all our energies rejoice as one;
And for this cause, perhaps, we angels find
Such strangeness in the music of mankind,
As draws us still to hear them when we can
And wonder at God's ways and ends in Man.

Yet men in the Great Music, I surmise
Must also share, for what in reveries,
In separateness, in silence they create,
They only play if they participate.
These six girls and their master play as one
Perfected creature; in that unison
They touch, at least, the state in which we move:
A mutual ecstasy of consenting love.

V. CODA

This love, which opened in sonata form
For these two solo instruments alone,
Began *fugato*, in a minor key;
Subject and answer, challenge and the calm
Sad, questing melody probed towards unknown
Diminished thirds that spoke for you and me.

And though their end we hardly yet surmise,
We took this as the statement of a theme
In which each bore an equal part, where each,
Like earth and heaven caused a sun to rise
Out of the dark foredawning of our dream
And brought its jubilant noon within our reach.

But with the second subject, what we thought
Improvisation, impromptu at the least,
Led into a full symphony. We found
Ourselves, in those imperious energies caught
And caught up. Could our prelude have released
This mastering, terrifying tide of sound?

Its battering fugue drowns ours; in that eclipse
Chords are articulate spirits more real than we;
Archangels of sound sweep through us to evoke
For us the temporal world's apocalypse
And, as we merge in its entelechy
Its trumpets tear us like a lightning stroke.

What we had thought our pure, complete design,
We glimpse as random phrases, swept along
Into those hurricane harmonies, our two
Chance instruments mere notes in the divine
Rage of a cosmos rapt in its own song,
Allegro, allegro molto!—Yes, but who,

What then is the composer? How and why
Were we two chosen to set his forces free?
... Listen! His second movement has begun:
Transfigured, exalted, radiant, you and I
Emerge in one grave, soaring melody,
Lento e sostenuto; one by one

All voices of the universal frame
Join in and swell that great polyphony.
There sounds the answer, though we could not know
Till this vast, triumphing andante came
Like some calm estuary widening to a sea
Which welcomes and contains its mighty flow.

Chosen, subsumed, translated by such powers
And purpose as we could not understand,
How should we question, how challenge what is done?
And still, we know this music is not ours;
Lost to our own and to each other we stand
For his last movement, that unrisen sun,

Not facing towards the splendour still to come
Heralded by this march of rising chords
Which fill all space with their superb design,
But back to where we touched in our small room,
Looked, listened and knew without the help of words
That I was then your music and you mine.

VIVALDI, BIRD AND ANGEL

NOTES

Vivaldi, known as the Red Priest, perhaps on account of his flaming red hair, was born probably about 1677, son of a famous violinist in Venice. Ordained a priest in 1703, he was prevented by a chest complaint from carrying out his office. He began to teach at the *Ospedale della Pietà* in 1703 and, with some intervals, continued to compose and teach there until his death about 1741. The six flute concertos (Opus 10) were published at Amsterdam in 1728 and are often mentioned as the first examples of instrumental music written for a solo instrument throughout, with the other instruments as a background. I have arbitrarily taken one of these, which Vivaldi called *Il Cardellino* (The Goldfinch), as the first of the group.

The *Ospedale della Pietà* was one of four foundling hospitals maintained by the State of Venice. At the beginning of the eighteenth century it had become primarily an advanced school of music in which foundling girls and others who showed an aptitude for music were educated under the leading masters of the day. They wore scarlet religious habits but were not professed and the young men of Venice frequented their concerts in the hope of obtaining wives. As performances were ordinarily held on Sundays in the chapel the audience were unable to applaud in the usual way in the sacred premises and did so by clearing their throats, coughing and scraping their feet. The most able girls, rarely over the age of twenty, were accorded special conditions and the rank of *Maestra privilegiata*. A picture by Guardi in the Munich Pinakothek shows them at a public concert in the *Sala dei Filarmonici* performing in 1782, before a visiting Russian Grand Duke. In Venetian dialect they were called *ospealiere*.

Monteverdi (1567-1643), at St Marks in Venice, was one of the first composers to write music for instruments in their own right instead of treating them as replacement for voices and limited to the range and practice of vocal music. Ludovico Zacconi, a Venetian monk and composer, in 1596 laid down the rule that the human pulse was the true measure of time in music, but between 1696 and 1732 a number of French inventions substituted pendulum devices, forerunners of the modern metronome, for this purpose. The flute in the early eighteenth century was usually made of boxwood, in four sections and coloured dark red, unlike the modern metal instruments. It was also a more primitive instrument and could only be used outside certain keys with a good deal of rather precarious cross-fingering. "Cembalo" was the usual Italian name for the harpsichord at this period.

The goldfinch is a strikingly beautiful bird with crimson face backed by black and yellow behind the eyes and golden, barred wings. They have a characteristic and charming song. The two sexes have the same colour and markings. They belong to the very few species of birds which appear to have a musical range and structure of song comparable to human music and to sing for pleasure as well as for sexual display and courtship. They mate in spring and usually have a second brood in summer.

The attributes of angels I have adopted, with some additions of my own, from St Thomas Aquinas.

A.D.H.